This picture book helps children learn about mathematical concepts through a colorful and entertaining story.

Math concepts explored may include:
• Understanding math concepts
• Numbers and operations
• Dealing with operations with mathematical signs ($\div$, $\times$, $+$, $-$): multiplication

About the Author
Eun-sun Han studied child psychology and education at Sungkyunkwan University in Seoul, South Korea, and now works as an author and pediatric psychotherapist. She got the inspiration for this book after reading an article about people involved in the Build Birdhouses Campaign.

Author's Note: Eun-sun Han notes it is not ecologically possible for various species of birds to live in the same habitat as they do in this story.

About the Illustrator
Ju-kyoung Kim became a professional illustrator after studying design in college. She has created artwork for many picture books. Ju-kyoung received an award from the 2006 Norma Picture Book Contest for *The Flying Birds*.

Tan Tan Math Story **The Flying Birds**

Original Korean edition © Yeowon Media Co., Ltd

This U.S edition published in 2015 by TANTAN PUBLISHING INC, 4005 W Olympic Blvd, Los Angeles, CA 90019-3258

U.S and Canada Edition © TANTAN PUBLISHING INC in 2015

ISBN: 978-1-939248-05-3

Printed in South Korea at Choil Munhwa Printing Co., 12 Seongsuiro 20 gil, Seongdong-gu, Seoul.

The Flying Birds

Written by Eun-sun Han   **Illustrated by Ju-kyoung Kim**

TanTan Publishing

One spring day, an old carpenter was walking through the park. The birds that noticed him flew away. They followed the rays of sunlight and then fluttered down, coming to rest on tree branches. The old man listened closely to the birds singing. Many years before, when he was young, he had listened happily to birds sing in much the same way.

The next morning, the old
carpenter started to make
something special. He measured
wood, cut it, drilled holes in it, and
sanded it smooth. He hummed
quietly as he worked, pouring his
whole heart into the effort.

The old carpenter made two small, beautiful birdhouses. He hung them in an old tree in the woods. And then he waited patiently. . . .

Time passed, and at last a pair of chickadees flew to the woods one day, raising their voices in song. A few days later, a pair of warblers arrived, softly waving their tails.

If there are 2 birds of each species and 2 birdhouses
(2 birds times 2 houses), there are 4 birds altogether.

$2 \times 2 = 4$

$2 \times 2 = 2 + 2$

The old carpenter was happy to see and hear the birds! He quickly made three more birdhouses. He made each of them a different shape, and then he decorated all of them. The old carpenter was pleased with the birdhouses, but he wondered whether the birds would like them.

Soon, a pair of jays flew to the woods, whistling. A pair of cute little nuthatches came, too. Then a pair of sparrows flew by to see the birdhouses.

If there are 2 birds of each species in each birdhouse and there are 3 birdhouses (2 birds times 3 birdhouses), there are 6 birds altogether.

$2 \times 3 = 6$

$2 \times 3 = 2 + 2 + 2$

The birds were busy all day every day. They brought grass and twigs to their new homes, which they used to build nests. Soon, the female chickadee laid three eggs. The female warbler also laid three eggs.

If there are 3 eggs in each birdhouse and there are 2 birdhouses, there are 6 eggs in total.

$3 \times 2 = 6$

$3 \times 2 = 3 + 3$

The female jay, nuthatch, and sparrow laid 4 eggs each. The old carpenter was amazed by and thankful for all the activity—and for the chicks that would soon hatch!

If there are 4 eggs in each nest and there are 3 birdhouses (4 times 3), there are 12 eggs in total.

$$4 \times 3 = 12$$
$$4 \times 3 = 4 + 4 + 4$$

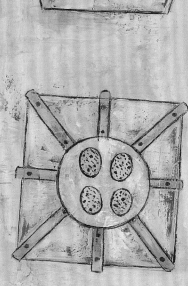

Day by day, the number of birds grew.
The woods were filled with their singing.

Bang, bang, bang, bang!

The old carpenter was hard at work. He made four two-story houses with two holes in each to welcome more birds that would come live—and sing—happily together.

If there are 2 holes in each birdhouse and there are
4 birdhouses (2 times 4), there are 8 holes altogether.

$2 \times 4 = 8$

$2 \times 4 = 2 + 2 + 2 + 2$

Soon, there was a pair of woodpeckers, kissing tenderly, in each of the holes in the two-story birdhouses.

If there are 2 birds in each hole and there are 8 holes (2 times 8), there are 16 birds in total.

$$2 \times 8 = 16$$

$$2 \times 8 = 2 + 2 + 2 + 2 + 2 + 2 + 2 + 2$$

Suddenly, the old carpenter had a brilliant idea. He got busy!

Bang, bang, bang, bang!

The carpenter made three three-story houses. Each birdhouse had three holes in it.

If there are 3 holes in each house and 3 birdhouses (3 times 3), there are 9 holes in total.

$$3 \times 3 = 9$$

$$3 \times 3 = 3 + 3 + 3$$

The carpenter hung the new birdhouses in the park. Many, many birds came to build nests there.

If there are 2 birds in each of the 9 holes (2 times 9), there are 18 birds in total.

$$2 \times 9 = 18$$

$$2 \times 9 = 2 + 2 + 2 + 2 + 2 + 2 + 2 + 2 + 2$$

The birds passed the seasons and raised their chicks in the birdhouses. The old carpenter's cozy houses sheltered them from wind and rain. The birds were busy, though sometimes they rested briefly. They often stayed put for a long while. Other times, they flew south for the winter but returned to the woods in the spring.

The old carpenter is still busy making birdhouses.
He is happy to hear the birds sing while he
works—and sometimes he sings with them!

Multiplication Is Repetition of Addition

Multiplication makes it easier to calculate quickly when adding the same numbers repeatedly. To learn multiplication, it's important to be familiar with adding groups of numbers. For example, if there are 3 groups of 5 (3×5), the total, or product, is 15. The result is the same as adding 5 three times (5 + 5 + 5). Multiplying 3×5 is also the same as adding 5 + 5 + 5, and the total for both operations is 15.

Through these processes, children can learn how multiplication works. When explaining the concept of "times" for the first time, it can help to demonstrate mathematical thinking by personalizing examples, for instance: "Your feet have grown three times bigger than they were when you were a baby," or "You are two times heavier now than you were when you were one year old."

Multiplication tables—which are sometimes the first thing people think of when multiplication is mentioned— are often considered a tool that makes multiplication easier. The ability to understand the general concept of multiplication, however, is more important than learning to make quick calculations. Requiring students to memorize multiplication tables is not the only approach for helping them understand and apply the concept.

Who Has More Eggs?

| **Activity Goal** | To understand the concept of multiplication by adding groups of numbers
| **Materials** | 2 pieces of drawing paper, crayons, paint, paintbrush, palette for mixing paint, bowl, scissors

1 Draw 13–15 round eggs of similar size on each drawing paper.

2 Decorate each egg with paint. Use a variety of patterns and colors, and allow the eggs to dry. Then cut out the eggs.

3 Gather all the eggs in a pile. The winner of a Rock, Paper, Scissors session takes 3 eggs from the pile and says: "One group of 3 is 3 ($1 \times 3 = 3$)."

4 Repeat the Rock, Paper, Scissors action. Each time the winner takes the eggs, he or she says: "One group of 3 is 3 ($1 \times 3 = 3$), 2 groups of 3 is 6 ($2 \times 3 = 6$), 3 groups of 3 is 9 ($3 \times 3 = 9$)—until they reach the total they have accumulated.

5 Play until there are no more eggs left in the pile. The person with the most eggs is the winner. When repeating the game, change the number of eggs drawn from the pile to 2 or 4.

Note: *This game is intended for 2 to 4 players. If more children will play the game, increase the number of eggs.*

Birdhouses for the Condominium Complex

The old carpenter is making another birdhouse. It is for birds living in a condominium complex. More birds should mean more happy singing!

If there are 2 holes in each house and 4 birdhouses (2 times 4 is 8), there are 8 holes in total.

$2 \times 4 = 8$

$2 \times 4 = 2 + 2 + 2 + 2$

If 2 birds live in each of the 8 holes (2 times 8),
16 birds have a new home!

$2 \times 8 = 16$

$2 \times 8 = 2 + 2 + 2 + 2 + 2 + 2 + 2 + 2$

A Happy Walk

The hardworking carpenter went out for a walk early one morning. Follow him on his nature walk in the woods.

There are 3 groups of 5 wildflowers each, which makes 15 wildflowers in total.

$3 \times 5 = 15$

$3 \times 5 = 3 + 3 + 3 + 3 + 3$

There are 2 groups of 3 eggs each, which makes 6 eggs in total.

$2 \times 3 = 6$

$2 \times 3 = 2 + 2 + 2$

There are 2 groups of 2 baby rabbits each, which makes 4 baby rabbits in total.

$2 \times 2 = 4$

$2 \times 2 = 2 + 2$

There are 3 groups of 4 mushrooms each, which makes a total of 12 mushrooms under the tree.

$3 \times 4 = 12$

$3 \times 4 = 3 + 3 + 3 + 3$

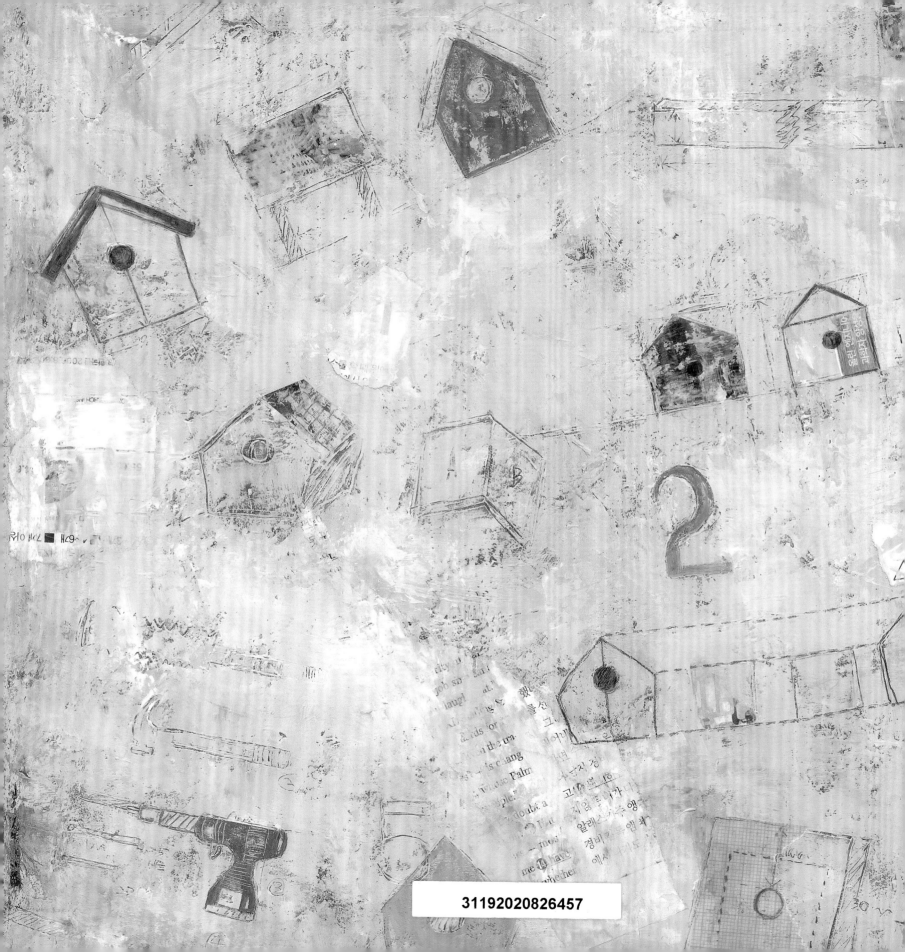